P.S. You Are Amazing

Written by Emma Meyer

Illustrations by Gabriella Shcherban

Production management by Magdalene Ward

For information address LittleBigPage, 312 W. 2nd St #1934
Casper, WY 82601, United States.

Paperback ISBN: 9788367973809

First Edition

P.S. YOU ARE Amazing

EMMA MEYER

You can **download the free audiobook** version of this book.

Go to the *last page* for more information!

Contents

CHAPTER 1

Nora Does Know Best

NORA LOOKED AT THE POPULAR GIRLS in her class, sighed, then slouched over her desk. Those girls—Scarlett, Rochelle, and Emilia—seemed to find everything so easy. Their hair was never out of place, they didn't trip over their own feet, and they always managed to say the right thing at the right time.

She daydreamed—as she often did—about being a shiny, popular, cool version of herself. She was so caught up in this thought that her elbows slipped out from under her, causing her chin to slam onto the desk with an unglamorous *thud*.

The entire class turned and looked at her, including her crush, Elijah, who she was pretty sure didn't even know her name.

Blushing, she sat up and tried not to make eye contact with anyone. Only, this didn't work as she managed to stare straight at a smirking Scarlett Valentine, who mouthed, *"Loser!"*

When the bell rang, Nora rushed outside to join her friends Leah and Zara. She was trying to shove the totally embarrassing moment in class from her mind when Zara waved her cell phone in her face.

Nora looked at it and her heart slumped. It was a post on one of Scarlett's social media pages—she was having a birthday party and had tagged all the popular kids as her way of an invite. Unsurprisingly, Nora, Leah, and Zara weren't invited, but their friend Zac was.

Zara looked at the post again, then, smirking at Zac, said, "Oh, it's pink themed. Do you need to borrow a sweater?"

"Nah, I own a pink shirt I can wear. Guys can pull off pink, too, you know." He pretended to look offended.

"Didn't Scarlett have a pink-themed party when she was seven? Maybe she has some leftover balloons she needs using up." Leah laughed.

"It's a pink *and lilac* theme, didn't you guys read it properly?" Zac asked.

Leah rolled her eyes. "No, duh. Us ordinaries weren't invited."

As her friends carried on talking, Nora gnawed on her fingernails while she thought about how unfair not being invited to the party was.

She didn't understand how Leah and Zara were fine

with being left out. Her friends were right, Scarlett did have a pink-themed seventh birthday party. Back then, they'd all been invited, and Nora had worn a pale pink tutu dress. She'd felt like a princess that day, but now she felt like a nobody . . . a loser.

She knew all too well that now—in ninth grade, not first—friendship dynamics had changed, and popular girls like Scarlett did not invite nerdy, awkward, ordinary girls like Nora Reeves to their parties.

Nora spent the rest of the day in a daydream of what ifs. What if she were prettier, less fidgety, slimmer, shorter, taller, sportier, smarter, chattier, cooler—would she get an invite then? The what ifs zoomed around her mind like out-of-control frisbees and would not leave her alone.

Later that day, as she walked home trailing behind her friends, her phone beeped. She looked at the message in disbelief. It was from an unknown number and said:

Nora, want to come to Scarlett's party? Complete three simple challenges and the invite's all yours. Reply yes if you're in.

Nora read and reread the message. She had no idea who it was from, but she told herself this didn't matter. Readjusting her tortoiseshell glasses, she read it one last time, typed *yes*, but didn't hit send.

She looked at her friends who were waiting for her by the school gate and considered talking to them about it.

"Hurry up, slowpoke," Leah teased.

Nora sighed and slipped her cell into her pocket. Some things were best kept a secret.

"You seem distracted. What's wrong?" Zara asked. "You're not still upset about Scarlett's party, are you?"

"No." Nora shook her head. "Of course not."

She grimaced at her own lie. She loved her friends, but she was sure that they wouldn't understand why being invited to Scarlett's party was so important to her.

Her cell phone felt like a great weight in her pocket, and suddenly, on worrying that replying to the message came with a time limit, she quickly pulled it out and hit reply.

At first, nothing happened, and Nora feared that it was a mistake, a joke, or something worse. On walking into class the next morning, she was sure Scarlett and her friends would laugh at her, but they didn't. None of the popular kids seemed to notice her at all, just like usual.

She checked her cell quickly before sliding it into the front of her backpack just as the teacher entered the room. Throughout class, she wondered if the mystery number would reply.

Then, during lunch, when she was walking out of the bathroom, she checked her cell and saw it there on her screen:

Challenge 1: Association is everything! Publicly ditch your uncool friends.

Nora felt terrible. She didn't want to ignore her friends, but she really wanted a party invite. As she walked into the cafeteria and saw her friends waving at her from their usual table, she hesitated.

She turned around and walked over to an empty table by the window, making sure her back was to them so she didn't have to see their disappointed looks. Eating lunch alone was no fun, and without the distraction of her friends, she was certain everyone was staring at her and secretly calling her a loser.

With just half of her sandwich eaten, she rushed out of there, avoiding her friends' confused glances at all costs. She felt terrible for ignoring them, but the party invite was just too tempting.

She spent the rest of lunch pacing the hallways and trying not to look so alone. She went back and forth to her locker and moved her books around just so she looked like she was doing something. On the third time of doing this, she closed her locker door and saw Scarlett, Rochelle, and Emilia—all of them looking effortlessly perfect as they stared at their cell phone screens.

Nora chewed on her lip and imagined what it would feel like to be like them, instead of like her. Scarlett and her friends never had juice stains on their shirts or scuff marks on their boots. They also never seemed to be alone—kids always flocked to them like crows to shiny things.

"Maybe one day things will change," Nora whispered to herself as she shuffled to class.

That's when her phone screen flashed and a new message from the mystery number appeared:

Challenge 2: Don't be such a Goody Two-shoes. Reputation is important, so show your rebellious side in the next class.

Nora didn't like getting into trouble. The last time a teacher had scolded her for passing notes in class—a note Emilia was sending to Rochelle, but landed on her desk by mistake—she had almost cried.

On seeing Leah and Zara walk into class, she quickly looked at her desk and avoided eye contact. She feared they would come over and ask her why she was being weird, the mystery message sender would find out and get mad, and . . . *argh!* Thankfully, Mrs. Day, her English teacher, appeared before this could happen.

As the class went on, Nora stared at the clock by the door and watched her chance to get a party invite tick away like the time left in the period.

She felt so jittery with nerves that she discreetly started

doodling on a piece of paper to try and calm herself. Unfortunately, she wasn't as discreet as she thought she was, because as she drew a flower with heart-shaped leaves, she heard Mrs. Day cough to clear her voice.

She looked up and Mrs. Day's scrunched-up face glared down at her. "Miss Reeves, does Emily Dickinson's innovative use of syntax bore you?"

Nora felt sick with dread and opened her mouth to mutter an apology. Only, as she started to splutter, she remembered that her time was running out to complete the second challenge, so instead, said, "Um, yes. They're boring and confusing, and I don't care."

The other kids in class giggled, her friends looked surprised with mouths open and eyes wide, and Mrs. Day arched her eyebrows in fury. Nora felt like she'd left her body and was watching a stranger sitting at her desk. She never answered back to anyone, and what she said about Emily Dickinson wasn't even true. She actually thought her poetry was innovative and soulful.

Mrs. Day ordered her to go to the principal's office, so Nora shoved her books into her backpack and stormed out of the room. As she marched along the empty hallway, her heart fluttering in her chest, she couldn't believe what she'd just done.

She sat on one of the hard chairs outside the principal's office and sneakily checked her cell. A new message had come up with:

Challenge 3: Your clothes are gross. Ditch the lame look and change your style.

Nora stared down at her pleated brown skirt and plain shirt and thought that maybe the mystery message sender was right. Her look was lame!

That evening at home, she waited until her older sister went downstairs, then she tiptoed into her room and "borrowed" a striped sweater and a pair of ripped jeans. The next morning, she woke up extra early so she could apply shimmery eyeshadow and vivid red lip gloss, curl her long brown hair, and leave the house before her sister spotted her.

She arrived at school hugging her backpack and feeling like a fraud. As she reached her locker, there was a note stuck to it with her name written on it. She pulled it free, hoping more than anything that this was the invite of her dreams. She opened the note and saw the capitalized word written in pink ink: *LOSER!*

Laughter sounded behind her, and with teary eyes, she turned to see Scarlett there—a sparkly vision of pastel blue—as she filmed her on her cell phone.

"Thanks for the laugh, Nora." She grinned. "But *my* party has a strict no desperate losers policy!"

Nora wanted the floor to open up and suck her in, but it didn't, so she pushed past Scarlett and her friends and rushed to the bathroom. As she leaned against the stall door, using big wads of toilet paper to blow her nose, a knock startled her.

"Nora, it's us. Please let us in," Leah said worriedly.

Nora thought they would be mad at her for ignoring them, but still, she sniffed and then opened the door.

"Whoa! You look terrible!" Zara exclaimed as she flung her arms around her friend. "Is that your sister's vampish lip gloss?"

Nora laughed and sobbed at the same time. Then, after apologizing, she explained to her friends about the secret challenges and all the stupid things she did to try to get a party invite.

"Nora, you were an idiot, but you're our friend and we love you," Leah told her.

"But please lose the crazy makeup, it's sooo not you." Zara chuckled as she led Nora over to the mirror and passed her a tissue.

Nora looked at her reflection—a makeup-smudged face and swollen red eyes—and felt like a clown. As she wiped off the bright colors, she asked her friends, "Why aren't you upset that Scarlett didn't invite you to her party?"

Leah shrugged. "Um! 'Cause she's a mean girl."

"Yeah, her party sounds like a form of torture." Zara shuddered.

"B-but, Zac's invited," she stammered.

"So what?! Zac is friends with everyone. He can go if he wants to. But I'm not bothered about Scarlett's stupid party." Leah nodded for clarification.

"Hey, let's have our own party at my house," Zara suggested.

"Oooh, that's a great idea. I'll bring popcorn and nail polishes," Leah added.

"Come here," Zara said as she turned Nora to face her and then applied some powder and some clear lip gloss. "Yep! Much more you."

Leah passed Nora her oversized hoodie to wear. It was much more Nora's style and covered some of the rips in her jeans. Then, with her arms linked with her friends, they left the bathroom and walked along the hallway.

Scarlett and her friends weren't there anymore, but Nora realized that their opinions didn't matter, and she no longer wanted to go to the party. She may not have been one of the cool kids, but this didn't change the fact that she had amazing friends who were there for her, even when she did dumb things.

As Nora closed her locker door, she saw Elijah walking toward her, his hair floppier and eyes shinier than usual. She expected him to walk right past her without even noticing that she existed, but instead, he smiled at her and said, "Hey, Nora."

OMG! He knows my name! she squealed to herself. She stared open-mouthed at her friends, who subtly waited until Elijah was out of earshot before grabbing Nora's hands and excitedly leaping into the air.

Nora couldn't believe it, but seeing how happy her friends were for her made her feel even better. She couldn't wait for the party later at Zara's house. It wouldn't be full of popular kids, but it would be with her two favorite people, and to her, that was all that mattered.

P.S.

I used to look at the popular kids and think that being like them would fix everything. In their world, everything seemed effortless. So, I thought that if I looked cooler, acted braver, or wore the right clothes, maybe I'd finally belong. But trying to change who I was only left me feeling like a joke—and worse, I almost lost my favorite people. The people who were with me through the good and bad times and actually cared about me.

Here's what I learned: Real friends don't need you to be shinier or braver or prettier. They just want you. The goofy, messy, awkward you. And that's enough.

Use your energy wisely, and not on people who only want to be around you when it's convenient for them. Instead, hold on tight to the ones who stick by you no matter what. These are your people, and they are where happiness lives.

Keep shining,
Nora

CHAPTER 2

Rochelle's Emotion Notion

ROCHELLE LISTENED TO MUSIC AS she danced around her room, shoving her homework, cheerleading uniform, swimsuit, snacks, and water bottle into her various bags. She was about to double-check she had everything when her backpack strap slipped off her arm and knocked over the photo frame on her desk.

She gasped and immediately froze. Even though the music kept playing, her mind fell silent. She picked up the photo and looked at the picture taken a few years ago. In it, she was all smiles as she posed with Grandma Ada in front of a rosebush.

"Sorry, Grandma," Rochelle whispered as she straightened the frame.

She didn't feel like dancing anymore. In fact, she wished she could roll into her bed and stay there all day. Grandma Ada had passed away last month, and ever since, Rochelle felt as though she was being followed around by a cloud of sadness. She'd tried shrugging away these feelings, but it didn't work. She'd also tried ignoring them, but that didn't seem to work either.

Rochelle hated feeling this way. She was far too busy to feel anything other than perfect. She dreamed of studying at Yale University, and as such, made sure she was a member of an eclectic mix of clubs to complement her high grades. She had a club for every day of the week—sometimes two—including swimming, cheerleading, photography, math league, dancing, and debate.

She thrived in her busy, fast-paced schedule and executed everything with expert precision. Rochelle was never late for anything, nor did she ever hand in her homework late or let her grades slip. At least, this is how it used to be, but ever since her grandma passed away, Rochelle had struggled to get out of bed, let alone focus on anything.

This was why she was running late this morning. She had buried herself beneath her blanket in the hope that the pit of sadness she felt in her stomach would go away. It didn't; instead, it only grew worse.

As her mom shouted for her to hurry up so she didn't miss the bus, she looked again at the photo, briefly remembering happier times. Then she grabbed her bags and rushed out of the room. She failed to notice that still on her bed—next to her hairbrush and a clear lip gloss—was her history homework.

On the bus, Rochelle stared at the blue stripes on her sneakers as she wiggled her feet. She tried to concentrate on her schedule, but all she could think about was her grandma and how she'd missed her last birthday dinner due to debate club commitments.

"Hey, Rochelle. Um, didn't you wear those leggings yesterday?" Her friend Scarlett frowned as she sat next to her.

Rochelle followed her gaze to her peach-colored leggings. The same leggings she'd worn the previous day, and then completely forgotten about.

She quickly tried to cover the yogurt stain she'd made from yesterday's lunch—proof she wasn't herself as she never usually looked anything less than perfect.

"Um, no. These are a different pair," she mumbled.

"I know they're not." Scarlett rolled her eyes. "Are you okay? It's not like you to make fashion errors."

"Yeah, fine." She forced a smile. "I just didn't sleep very well. My brother was snoring—it's so noisy I'm surprised he doesn't wake up the entire neighborhood."

Scarlett giggled and changed the subject, but Rochelle wasn't listening. She couldn't believe she'd worn dirty leggings in front of Scarlett, the style queen. Rochelle was certain she'd thrown them in the laundry basket, but she had been distracted last night. She'd been looking for her headphones when she found the trinket dish she'd made for her grandma in art club, but forgotten to give her.

Just thinking about this made her eyes well up, and she quickly wiped them on her shirt sleeve.

"Ro, are you sure you're okay?" Scarlett looked at her with concern. "It wasn't what I said about your leggings, was it? Peach is very in right now, so you can totally get away with wearing them twice in a row."

Rochelle managed a smile, knowing full well her friend didn't think this at all; she was just trying to be nice—at least in her own way.

"I've just been . . ." Rochelle started, deciding it was time to tell someone how she was feeling. Only, as she was talking, Scarlett stared out the window and gasped.

"Oh-em-gee, that woman's hat is disgusting! Someone needs to arrest her for crimes against fashion." She made a retching sound. "Ro, what were you saying?"

"It doesn't matter," Rochelle muttered. She told herself it was better if she kept her feelings to herself, especially as she thought they were really stupid.

Her family was coping just fine after Grandma's death. They didn't get upset at the smallest of things like she did, so she didn't think she had a good reason to feel this way.

As she walked along the school hallway, all she could think about was how she couldn't remember the last time she'd told her grandma that she loved her. What if her grandma had passed away thinking that she didn't care about her? The thought of never being able to tell her how she felt nagged away at her as she rummaged through her locker, and distracted her so much, she forgot to take out her history textbook.

In class, as she searched through her backpack and noticed that both her homework and textbook were missing, a sense of doom hit her. *Oh no!* Her teacher seemed unimpressed with her mumbled response and walked away from her desk before she finished talking.

Rochelle felt like the whole class was laughing at her and thinking that she was a failure. She tightened her ponytail, straightened her shoulders, and fixed a smile on her face. On the outside, she looked her normal, assertive self, but on the inside, she felt as wobbly and unstable as Jell-O.

After that, Rochelle's week went from bad to worse. In the swimming tournament, she miscounted her backstrokes and collided with the wall with such force that she gave herself a concussion and had to be helped out of the water. Even through her blurred vision, she could sense her team's livid glances at her—they were winning until she had messed up.

During cheerleading practice, she was balancing in the middle of the pyramid when she thought back to the last time her grandma had cuddled her and felt the tears form in her eyes. Without thinking, she went to wipe them onto the back of her hand. She wobbled and tumbled forward, causing the entire pyramid to topple over, including the girls above her, who then shot her daggers for the rest of the day.

In debate club, all she could think about was how sad she felt, and her mind went completely blank. Everyone in the club was staring at her, and she heard some of them *tsk*. She felt so humiliated, she ran out of the room and vowed never to return.

Then, in photography club, she walked into the dark-room and, without thinking, flipped the light switch on. This ruined all of the negatives being developed, and also got her chucked out because Vera, the club president, thought she did it on purpose.

All of these instances bubbled up in Rochelle's mind until she couldn't take it anymore. Her cell wouldn't stop beeping, but she didn't care. She just wanted the whole wide world to leave her alone.

She marched into her bedroom, slammed her cell phone into her laundry basket, grabbed the picture of her with Grandma Ada, sank onto her bed, and burst into tears.

There was a gentle knock on the door, and her mom peeked her head around it. Seeing how upset Rochelle was, she hurried over to her and hugged her close.

"I just miss her so much," Rochelle sobbed.

"Oh, sweetie, it's okay. I miss her too." Mom teared up.

When Rochelle was able to, she told her mom about her awful week and how sad she felt all of the time.

"I just wish I'd seen Grandma more. I don't want her to be mad at me," she said with a quivering voice.

"Sweetie, Grandma loved you very much and would never want you to be upset. I have these doubts all the time—that I should have done more. But I know Grandma wouldn't want me to feel like this."

"No, Mom, she'd want you to be happy."

Mom managed a smile. "She'd want us both to be happy."

Rochelle knew her mom was right, but it was still hard to shake away her sadness.

That weekend, she and her mom went to Grandma's gravestone and left flowers there—pink roses and coneflowers, her favorites.

At home, they made a memory box together out of an old shoebox. They covered it in floral paper and added items that reminded Rochelle of her grandma—a seashell they had collected together on the beach, the rock people they had made together when she was eight, and various birthday and good luck cards she'd given her over the years.

She was looking at the items when Mom pulled something out from behind her back: Grandma's green and blue silk scarf that she had worn all the time.

"I want you to add this to your box. Grandma would want you to have it." Mom smiled as she held it out.

Rochelle's eyes welled up and she tried to sniff back

her tears. Only, this time, they were happy tears. She felt touched that her mom would give her something so precious. Thanking her, Rochelle took the scarf and smelled it. Orange blossom. Grandma Ada's signature scent.

Rochelle's mom spoke to the school and arranged for her to see the school counselor to talk through her feelings. She'd only had a few sessions, but Rochelle found talking to someone about her emotions was helpful. Her counselor suggested she keep an emotion journal so she could track her daily mood and feelings.

He also suggested that she should confide in her friends—for her last two sessions, she'd told them she was studying in the library to avoid telling them the truth.

Rochelle knew her counselor was right, so after her third session, she found Scarlett and Emilia and blurted out, "I wasn't in the library. Since my grandma passed away, I've been struggling to cope with my emotions. I felt sad and guilty all the time. I told my mom, and now I'm seeing the school counselor. I'm sorry for not telling you both sooner. I just didn't understand my own feelings then, but I think I'm starting to now."

Her friends were silent at first, and Rochelle worried she had made a mistake in telling them. Then she saw them exchange a look, step forward, and wrap their arms around her.

No words were said, but in that moment, they weren't

needed. Rochelle felt the warmth in their actions. As she hugged them back, she realized that she wasn't alone and that she had people around her who cared about her.

There were still times when Rochelle had bad days, and she found herself missing Grandma Ada so much it ached. On these days, she and her mom would each think of a special memory about Grandma that made them smile.

"I loved how she always had cooking shows on in the background, even though I don't think she ever made any of the recipes from them." Rochelle chuckled.

"She knew so many names of flowers, even the almost-impossible-to-say Latin ones." Mom smiled fondly.

After that, Rochelle dropped her least favorite clubs so she could focus on her favorite ones and not overwhelm herself. Studies and clubs were important, but so was looking after herself and having fun with her friends.

Grandma Ada may not have been with them anymore, but Rochelle knew that she would always live on in their memories. No one ever truly left, not fully. Rochelle also knew that it was okay to feel sad sometimes and that grief for everyone looked and felt different. There was no right way to miss someone.

P.S.

I used to think being busy was the answer to everything—clubs, grades, goal perfection. If I kept moving, I could outrun the sadness that followed me around after Grandma Ada passed away. But this didn't work. Ignoring my feelings only made me burn out and crumble harder.

Here's what I've learned: It's okay to grieve, it's okay to feel sad, it's okay to need help, and it's okay to really, really miss someone.

Talking to my mom, my counselor, and even my friends reminded me that I don't have to carry these thoughts and feelings alone. Sharing memories of Grandma hurts sometimes, but it also makes me smile, because love doesn't end just because someone is gone.

So please, if you're hurting, don't bottle it up the way I did. Reach out, speak up, and give yourself space to feel. It doesn't make you weak—it makes you human.

Best wishes,
Rochelle

CHAPTER 3

Florence Feels the Fear

FLORENCE STARED AT THE ENORMOUS red stone building in front of her and gulped in fear. She wasn't just the new girl at Kent Bridge High School; she was also the new girl in the country. Two weeks ago, she was in her house in England, holding back tears as she swapped bracelets with her friends. Now she was in an unfamiliar, noisy, chaotic place where she felt like the odd one out.

She fiddled with her red and white friendship bracelet, which a friend had made her—the colors of the English flag to remember home.

"Here goes nothing," she whispered as she bravely climbed the steps toward the entrance.

Inside, students filled every hallway, and she didn't know where she was supposed to go.

Spotting a girl with a purple backpack—Florence's favorite color—she walked over to her and politely said, "Hello, I'm new here. Do you know where I need to go?"

The girl wrinkled her nose and replied, "Huh!"

Florence didn't understand what was going on at first, but then she thought that the girl probably didn't understand her accent.

"I'm . . . new," she said slowly. "Where . . . do . . . I—"

"Main office is that way." The girl waved her hand to the left and then walked off.

Florence spun her bracelet around her wrist several times and then took in a deep breath. It was hard enough being the new girl without having students look at her like an alien because of the way she spoke.

Feeling deflated, she shuffled her way to the main office and was given a schedule and directions to her homeroom.

Everything felt bigger here, and she felt like a tiny, confused, out-of-place speck in comparison. As she stared down at her long-sleeved shirt and jeans, she felt strange not being in a school uniform like she wore back in England.

It took her forever to find her classroom—there were just too many connecting hallways. Then, when she finally found it, she walked into a class packed full of students, and every single one of them stared at her.

The teacher introduced her to everyone—Florence was grateful she didn't make her speak in front of them—and then pointed her to an empty desk near the back.

Afterward, some girls came over to her and said they'd

walk with her to their next class. As Florence went to thank them, she found herself toning down her accent.

The girls seemed nice, and they invited Florence to sit with them at lunch. One of the girls, Emilia, arrived at the table with a basket of cheese fries—the trouble was, in England, they called them chips.

"Those chips look good," Florence said in her best non-English accent.

Emilia frowned at her and was about to say something, but Scarlett hit her arm and said, "Florence, they're sooo tasty. You should go order some."

Florence nodded and then joined the line. Only, when she asked for chips, the lunch lady passed her a packet of potato chips—or as Florence called them, crisps.

Her cheeks turned as red as her auburn-colored hair as she clutched the chips and walked back over to the table. Scarlett and Emilia both laughed and called her dumb. Florence felt embarrassed and more out of place than ever.

"You can have some of mine if you want." Emilia held out her basket of fries.

Florence shook her head. "No thanks, I don't fancy them anymore."

Scarlett and Emilia both burst out laughing. They'd never heard anyone use the word "fancy" before.

"It means to want something. We say it a lot in England," Florence explained.

"You're so funny. It's like you talk a completely different language." Scarlett snorted.

Florence faked a smile and tried to hide how awkward she really felt. She wanted to fit into her new school, not stand out. As the other girls talked about cheerleading and TikToks—two things Florence didn't care about at all—she feigned interest in them. She tried not to say anything that sounded British and continued to mask her accent.

Desperate to feel like a normal American teen, she invited Scarlett, Emilia, and Rochelle for a sleepover at her house. She thought it would be fine—these girls were popular, so hanging out with them would make her popular too, right?

She spent hours tidying her room and hiding anything that felt too English—posters of British bands, pictures of her friends from back home, and any books with UK-English spelled words.

She planned a fun time with games and movies, but all they wanted to do was film TikToks, make fun of other girls' clothing choices on social media, and gossip about kids from school she didn't know.

Florence sat on her bed and played with her bracelet as she filmed the other girls performing a TikTok dance.

"Stop shaking the camera," Emilia groaned at her. "Wobbly videos are sooo not cool."

Florence apologized in her English accent and quickly

corrected it. She held the phone as steady as she could until there was a knock on the door. To her utter horror, her mom walked in holding a tray of Florence's favorite—and very British—snacks.

"I thought you could give your new friends a taste of back home," Mom said as she passed the tray around them. "Our chocolate bars, oh sorry, I mean candy bars, are much tastier."

Florence stared at the selection of British candy, potato chips, and cookies and gripped her blanket from embarrassment. As soon as her mom left the room, the other girls laughed about how gross and weird the snacks were.

Feeling overwhelmed, Florence quickly said, "Be right back, I need the toilet."

This resulted in more laughter, and Florence smacked her palm against her face. She'd slipped up again . . . She kept forgetting a toilet was called a bathroom here.

As she walked back along the hallway, she heard them making fun of her.

"Hello, I'm Florence Kennedy. I'm from this fancy place called England, and I eat chips in the toilet," Scarlett mimicked Florence's fake accent.

"I'm Mrs. Kennedy, Florence's mum, and I hoard weird candy because I am so boringly British!" Emilia mocked.

As she walked back into the room, they all fell silent.

She wanted to call them out on their mean words, especially the ones they'd said about her mom, but she decided it was better to stay quiet.

The sleepover went from bad to worse, and Florence felt like she was there to be laughed at. Even though she kept up her fake accent and tried to just agree with what the other girls said, she saw them looking at each other and smirking and felt like she was the only one of them who didn't get the joke.

The next morning, after they made fun of the breakfast options—beans on toast, crumpets, and cereal brands they'd never heard of—the girls left, and Florence tidied up the kitchen with a sigh.

"Flo, I want you to be happy and to make new friends, but I don't like how you aren't yourself around those girls," her mom said in concern.

"I know." Florence sighed again and slumped into a chair. "I just wanted them to like me."

"I know being the new girl is hard, but I want them to like you for you. Not for whoever you're trying to be." Mom nodded. "You're wonderful, Florence, please don't ever forget that."

Looking at her mom, Florence knew she was right.

"I know, Mom—I mean Mum! I'll be me from now on," she said in her normal accent.

"Oh, good. You have such a lovely voice, you should never hide it, and please, always call me mum, not mom." She smiled.

As Florence rolled her eyes, she couldn't help but smile too. Pretending to be a different version of herself just to fit in led her to befriend girls who just made fun of her. She was proud of her roots, and she didn't want to pretend to be anything other than who she was.

The next day, at lunch, instead of sitting with Scarlett and her friends, she walked straight past their table and sat by herself instead. She kept her back to them as she loaded potato chips into her cheese sandwich to make a crisp butty, just like she made back home. Although she did feel a little lonely, she much preferred sitting by herself to feeling like she had to fake who she really was.

As she bit into her sandwich, a girl from class walked past and asked, "You put chips in your sandwich? Hmm, looks tasty."

After the last class of the day, Florence was packing her books when the same girl walked toward her.

"Hey, Florence, isn't it? I'm Nora." She smiled at her. "You're from England, right? Um, I bet you must miss it."

Florence was about to talk in her fake accent, but she stopped herself. She wasn't going to fake who she was anymore.

In her normal voice, she replied, "I do miss my mates back home, but I don't really miss the rain."

Nora didn't make fun of her; instead, she seemed genuinely interested in finding out more about Florence and asked her more questions. They walked out of class together, and as they continued chatting, for the first time since she'd started this school, Florence felt relaxed. It was a lot less tiring *not* having to fake anything about her.

Over the next few weeks, Florence grew closer to Nora and her friends. They never laughed at her when she used British words and instead seemed fascinated in the differences. They loved hearing that back home, sweaters were called jumpers, trash cans were called bins, and that people said "chuffed" when they were happy with something.

Over time, Florence began to feel as though she had a friendship group in her new school that she truly belonged in.

One day, Nora linked arms with her and said, "Hey, let's go and find our other mates and see if they wanna go to the diner after school."

"Sounds great. I think it might rain later, though," she replied.

"Just like England." Nora chuckled.

"Yep, sorry, I think I brought the weather with me."

"That's okay. The plants like it." Nora shrugged.

"Either way, I'm chuffed to just spend time with you guys. I used that word right, right?"

"Yep. You're now a British slang pro." Florence giggled.

As they walked along the hall, Florence continued to beam with happiness. She finally felt accepted for being her true, unique, one-of-a-kind self. English accent and all.

P.S.

When I first came to Kent Bridge High, I thought the only way to fit in was to hide everything that made me . . . me. I toned down my accent, pretended to like things I didn't, and even laughed along when people made fun of my favorite snacks. But the harder I tried to blend in, the lonelier I felt.

What I finally learned is this: Pretending doesn't win you real friends. The right people—the ones worth having—will like you for who you truly are, quirks, accent, and all. Being yourself may feel scary at first, but it's so much less exhausting than faking it. And when you do find friends who get you, it feels amazing.

So please don't hide the things that make you different. They're what make you shine.

Cheerio,
Florence

CHAPTER 4

Leah Fades the Filter

Leah curled up beneath her striped blanket and scrolled through her social media pages. As usual, they were full of perfect-looking girls. Ones who didn't have acne, greasy hair, or awkward smiles.

Looking at these images made her feel horrible. She didn't have perfect skin, shiny hair, or a cute smile, and she convinced herself that she wasn't as pretty as these girls and never would be. Despite how bad social media made her feel, scrolling through it was part of her nighttime routine.

Sometimes, Leah dreamed about being the prettiest girl in school—the kind who had cute boys flock to her, and who could wear any outfit and pose for any picture and always manage to look like a catwalk model.

Other times, she had nightmares, ones where she turned into this giant, gangly, hideous buck-toothed version of herself who the popular kids pelted their textbooks at as they chased her out of the school.

Even though social media made her feel this way, the fear of missing out on an oh-so-important post kept her scrolling. She looked at the perfect photos of other girls her age, and then read the comments saying how gorgeous and hot they were. No one ever said these things about her photos.

She was about to put her cell phone down and go to bed when she saw that her friend Zara had tagged her in a picture taken from their last sleepover—she was making a dorky face and a love heart with her fingers. Leah laughed; it was a funny picture taken from a great night.

As she read the comments, her stomach lurched. A boy from tenth grade that she didn't know had written:

Zara, what's with your ugly friend?

Ugly. The word whirled in her head like a spinning top. She tried to hold back her tears as she typed a frantic message to Zara asking her to remove the post. Before she'd had time to send it, the post was deleted, and a message from Zara popped up:

Leah, I'm sooo sorry. Ignore him, he's a massive loser.

Leah replied that it was okay, but in truth, it wasn't. All she could think about was that word, and that someone thought this was what she was. It didn't seem to matter that she didn't know who this boy was; his comment wouldn't fade from her mind.

She finally fell to sleep with that word repeating in her head: *Ugly! Ugly! Ugly!*

The next day at school, Leah wore a baggy hoodie and tried to blend into the background—not easy when she was the tallest girl in her grade. She saw groups of kids messing around and was convinced they had seen the comment and were laughing at her.

Ugly! Ugly! Ugly! She hated the word, but she couldn't shake it from her mind.

After school, Leah went to the mall with her friends, and still feeling down, she lingered behind them. Suddenly, Nora grabbed her arm and dragged her over to the water fountain for a picture. Leah panicked; she didn't want unflattering pictures of her posted again. She didn't have the strength left to deal with being called ugly again.

"That's such a cute pic of us all." Zara smiled, and the other girls gathered around her cell phone.

Leah stared down at it and just saw her tall frame, blotchy skin, and awkward expression.

"Please don't post it, I look gross." She fretted, fighting back tears.

"Give it here." Nora pulled the cell phone out of Zara's hand and fiddled with the filters. "We all look amazing, but I can make us look even better. How about cat ears?"

She waved the image at them; they now all had digital fluffy cat ears on their heads.

"Cute, but maybe we should try a different filter," Zara suggested.

Nora nodded, added a different filter, then grinned as she showed the others. Leah stared wide-eyed at the image. It was still her, but her skin was flawless, her hair shiny, and in it, the awkward expression she was making actually looked cute.

"Oooh, I like it. I want to show my friends in England," Florence cooed.

"So, I'm okay to post it like this?" Zara checked with everyone.

They all agreed, including Leah, who couldn't stop staring at the photo. By the time Leah arrived home, the picture had received fifty-five likes and a ton of comments saying, "Gorgeous girls," "Looking fab," and fire emojis.

That night, as Leah scrolled through her apps and saw the shiny, perfect pictures of other girls, she thought about what filters she could use to make herself look that good too. She stayed up late adding filtered versions to all of her stored photos, then she scrolled through them, telling herself that at least in cell phone world, she now looked pretty.

The next morning, as she brushed her teeth and looked in the bathroom mirror, she saw all of her flaws in their raw, makeup-free, blemished reality. She hated her filter-free image so much that she closed her eyes as she spat out the toothpaste. Then she covered her face with her hand so she wouldn't catch sight of her reflection again.

In reality, her skin didn't glow, her hair didn't sparkle, and her eyes didn't pop. When she looked at the real her, all she felt was ugly.

To avoid feeling this way, she opened her phone's camera, set it to her favorite filter, balanced it on her dresser, then applied her makeup without having to look at her unfiltered self.

She lived the rest of the day through filters, touching up her eyeshadow and styling her hair while using it. In the school yard, she held her cell up and watched the other students walk past in a perfect, shiny haze.

She wished more than anything that she could click her fingers and apply this filter to the real world, but she supposed that feeling good in this virtual cell phone world would have to do. At least there, she could make herself slimmer, shorter, and prettier. She loved looking at her shiny self and hated seeing her normal, flawed self.

That weekend, on the way to a family gathering, Leah wouldn't stop looking at her cell phone, even though her mom told her to stop. This resulted in her mom snatching it from her and putting it in her pocket. Although Leah groaned about this, she had a great time talking to her relatives without her filtered obsession distracting her.

Then her younger cousin, Callie, rushed over to her and snapped a picture of them both. Leah blinked and then stared at the photo.

"Oooh, we look great." Callie beamed.

"Let me see." Leah grabbed the phone out of her hand and stared at the unfiltered image in front of her. "Ugh! We both look really ugly. Delete it!"

Callie's smile vanished and she fought back tears as she rushed out of the room. Leah stared down at the photo on Callie's cell phone that she was still holding.

Her aunt peered over her shoulder and said, "That's a lovely picture of you both."

Leah was about to reply that it wasn't, but she stopped herself, and instead smiled and said, "Yep."

The more she looked at it, the more she realized that despite her flyaway hair and Callie's exaggerated grin, they both looked real. They both looked happy.

Leah knew she needed to make it up to Callie, so she took two pieces of cake up to her room. She found her lying in her den—made from a sideways chair and her bedpost—and crawled in after her.

"I grabbed you some cake before your greedy brothers gobbled it all," she said as she passed a plate to her.

"I'm not hungry," Callie murmured as she stared down at the fluffy pillow she was cuddling.

"I shouldn't have said we looked ugly. I didn't mean it. I've been so obsessed with filters and looking perfect that I forgot what being myself looked like," Leah admitted.

"So you don't think I'm ugly?" Callie asked.

"Nope! Trust me, Callie. You will never be ugly. Never ever, and well . . . I actually think the photo you took was great." She passed Callie her phone. "Now, are you sure you don't want cake? It's red velvet."

"Actually, yeah, maybe I do want cake." Callie smiled and then brought the plate toward her. "Leah, you will never be ugly either."

The two girls stuffed forkfuls of cake into their mouths and enjoyed hanging out together in the den. Leah loved spending time with her cousin without worrying about being perfect all the time. She didn't touch up her lip gloss or worry about her having messy hair.

For the rest of the gathering, Leah made the most of not having her cell on her and instead lived in the moment. Trying to be perfect all the time and hiding behind a filter was exhausting. Just being herself, flaws and all, and not worrying about them made life much more fun.

On the way home, when Leah's mom handed her cell phone back, she found herself scrolling on social media and seeing the shiny-looking people differently. They weren't real representations of themselves, but altered, fake versions.

Looking at the passing billboard, she saw a flawless woman in a bikini advertising sunscreen, and knew that the picture had been airbrushed. These altered images were everywhere. On TV, in movies, on TikTok, in music videos. The reality was that everyone had flaws and imperfections. Nobody was truly perfect looking, but it was these imperfections that made someone unique. She had tried so hard to look like these other girls, when in reality, these were edited versions of themselves.

Leah framed the photo of her and Callie and placed it on her desk to remind her that being happy was far more important than faking being perfect. She also embraced taking natural, real photos. She snapped pictures of her family and friends when they weren't expecting it, and the result was a montage of in-the-moment, authentic images.

She told her friends she didn't want photos of her to be filtered, and showed them how great unfiltered versions could be. It gave her a newfound love for taking photos, and she joined the school photography club.

These altered images were everywhere, and sometimes, Leah couldn't help but look at them and feel ugly in comparison. Whenever the word "ugly" popped into her head, she stood up straight, smiled, and silently said, "Leah Levine, you are *not* ugly. You are not fake. You are real. You are you."

In a world packed full of fakeness, Leah was finally okay with being her very real, not always shiny, a little bit flawed, genuine, and very happy self.

P.S.

For a long time, I thought filters made me prettier—and without them, I was just ... ugly. I scrolled past flawless photos online and convinced myself these were real representations of other girls my age, and I'd never measure up. But chasing "perfect" only made me miserable, and I forgot what real even looked like.

It took one unfiltered picture with my cousin to remind me: Happiness doesn't need editing. Real smiles, messy hair, and silly faces are worth more than fire emojis or fake perfection. Filters might hide flaws, but they also hide the truth—and the truth is, no one is flawless. Even perfect-looking influencers get bad hair days.

So if you ever feel like you don't look "good enough," remember this: You don't need a filter to shine. You're already beautiful, just as you are.

Always,
Leah

CHAPTER 5

Amara's Math Mare

Amara looked at her math homework and groaned. The squiggly lines and italic numbers made no sense to her whatsoever. It didn't matter that her teacher had explained it to her three times; the equations still confused her.

She had always found math difficult. Back when she was younger, teachers and her parents used candy and stickers to try and make math more fun. This usually led to her frustrated parents accusing her of not trying on purpose to get extra candy.

Now, at fourteen, there was nothing fun about math, and to Amara, it may as well have been in some ancient language.

The more she looked at her homework, the less she seemed to understand it. She twiddled her pen between her fingers and thought about knocking on her older brother Tyrone's door and asking him—he was a math whiz—but the last time she'd done that, he'd lost his patience and called her stupid.

There was absolutely no way she was going to ask her parents. Their days of trying to explain things to her with candy were long gone. Her dad was an engineer and her mom an accountant, so they found everything number related easy. They just couldn't understand why she found math so hard.

Sighing, she scribbled down some answers—it was mostly guesswork—then she grabbed a book, squished into her beanbag, and started reading. Caught up in the fictional world of mythical creatures and sorcerers, she began to relax. She much preferred words to numbers.

The problem was, her struggles with math didn't just stop at her homework. It affected a lot of different aspects of her life. Just that month, she'd gotten confused with the times on her schedule and walked into the completely wrong class, where a roomful of seniors had gawked at her.

Another time, when she tried to pay for her cheese fries, she realized she was short by twenty cents—she'd added up her money wrong. She held up the line rummaging through her backpack for change. Thankfully, her friend Reina appeared and gave her the money she needed.

Often, Amara was either super early or very late for events because she read the times wrong. Distances confused her, and she couldn't work out how long it would take for her to get from one place to another. She'd once caught the bus to 143rd Street, but hopped off at 134th by mistake. She tried walking it, but ended up more lost, and had to phone her brother to come and pick her up. He came, but for the entire drive back, he snorted at her and called her stupid.

She tried to understand math, she really did, but she just didn't. She wanted to be a writer, not a mathematician—an idea that her parents hated. In their eyes, this wasn't a proper job.

That week, Amara not only failed her math homework—her stomach dropped upon seeing the bright red F that seemed to glow on the page—she also messed up the math test she had spent days studying for. She was so nervous about making mistakes that she couldn't concentrate properly and scribbled answers down in a panic.

"This isn't good enough, Amara." Her teacher, Mrs. Ashley, scowled down at her as she placed her test results on her desk. "This is an important year, and I advise you to try harder."

Amara looked at her results: two out of twenty. The rest of the class snickered at her and she wished she could vanish into her chair.

On the way out of class, a boy walked past her and coughed, *"Stupid!"* His friends laughed, and she felt even worse.

Her friend Vera tapped her on the shoulder and said, "Ignore him, he's the stupid one. Seriously, he thinks wearing his T-shirts inside out actually looks cool."

Amara chuckled, even though inside, she felt like she was crumbling like a cookie.

As her friends went on about the school camping trip coming up, even though she'd been excited about it for weeks, all she could think about was math and how terrible she was at it. She wondered if she really was just stupid. No one else seemed to find math as hard as she did, and she felt terrible because of it.

Things nose-dived at home when on coming back from the bathroom, she saw her mom next to her open backpack, her math homework and test paper in her hands.

"Look at this." Mom shoved the papers into Amara's dad's hands. "Our daughter is underachieving."

Amara regretted not crumpling the papers up and placing them in the trash. She knew her parents would hold this against her forever.

"But Mom, I studied. I really did, I just—"

"Enough! Your brothers don't bring shame on us like this. Do you think they would let Jamel stay at Harvard if he were this lazy?" Mom shouted.

"No, but—"

"And Tyrone wouldn't be on track to get the highest GPA in the school if he moped around reading drivel all day." Her voice reached new octaves.

"But I tried. I just don't unders—"

"Amara, you're upsetting your mother. Is that what you want?" Dad asked in a quietly stern voice.

Amara saw the disappointment in his eyes and shook her head. She knew there was no point arguing with them. They found math super easy, so they just couldn't accept the fact that she didn't.

"You can forget about the camping trip. We're not rewarding you for your unacceptable efforts." Her mom refused to meet her gaze as she walked off.

"You must try harder, Amara. You can't carry on distressing your mother like this," Dad said before he strode off to his office.

Amara didn't sleep well that night. In her dreams, giant numbers followed her around like a flock of angry birds.

When her friends messaged about what they were packing for the camping trip, she ignored them and tried to distract herself by reading instead. Even that didn't work, as all she could think about was how much she'd disappointed her parents. She wasn't supersmart like her brothers, and she never would be. It felt so unfair.

The next day, she woke up with an anxious feeling swirling in her stomach at the thought of going to her math class. She worried about it so much that she thought she might vomit. Her friends told her to go to the school nurse, but she thought this would make things worse. If her parents found this out, they would accuse her of skipping class and be even madder at her.

She shuffled into math class and nervously took her seat. As she looked up, she noticed a woman she didn't recognize writing on the whiteboard. At first, she worried she had entered the wrong classroom, but she recognized the other classmates in there, so she knew this wasn't the case.

The woman introduced herself as Miss Jones and said she would be teaching them while their usual teacher was away. Amara sighed, anxious that this meant there was someone else she would disappoint.

As the class went on, she stared at the board and, despite her best efforts to listen, found herself daydreaming. The numbers just didn't make any sense. Miss Jones gave them problems to work on, then went around the class to check on everyone. When she reached Amara, she saw a blank page and asked what was wrong.

Amara was flustered. "I'm sorry, Miss Jones. It just doesn't make any sense to me."

The teacher nodded and then walked to the next student. Amara was glad she hadn't shouted at her, but she also felt sad that it seemed like the teacher had given up on her.

She doodled on her page as she told herself to just accept that things would never change. She would never understand math and, unlike her brainy brothers, would be a constant disappointment to her parents.

At the end of class, when Miss Jones asked Amara to stay behind, the other kids sneered and she felt certain she was about to get in *big* trouble. She wanted to run out of the room, but her friends gave her reassuring smiles and said they would wait for her outside.

Only, the teacher didn't shout at her. To Amara's surprise, she asked her what she found tricky about math. Amara explained that she muddled numbers in her head, she confused times, often miscounted change, and couldn't remember more than one number at a time.

The teacher smiled at her and in a friendly voice said, "I think you may have a condition called dyscalculia, which makes processing numbers difficult."

Amara had never heard of this before, and she felt a little scared that dyscalculia meant she had some awful, incurable disease. But as Miss Jones explained what it meant, it started to seem less frightening, and instead, made more sense, as though invisible dots were being connected in her mind.

Miss Jones said she would talk to the school's guidance counselor about it and try to get her some extra help.

For the first time ever, Amara actually felt listened to. She wasn't "stupid" or "lazy," she just needed to learn anything number related in a different way.

She started having extra lessons with a math tutor, who explained numbers to her in a way she could understand. He told her to keep a math journal so she could keep track of the calculation steps, and she was no longer afraid of admitting she didn't understand something.

Amara realized that her brain processed numbers differently from her friends, and that this was okay. The trouble was, her parents were having a hard time understanding this. They were convinced that she was using dyscalculia as an excuse for underachieving.

In her next tutor session, all she could think about was how her parents didn't believe her, and it meant she couldn't concentrate properly. When her tutor asked what was wrong, she explained this to him.

"You could always try explaining how you feel to them in a different way. Maybe you could use your creative side," he suggested.

Amara thought this was a great idea, so she spent all of her spare time writing a story with hand-drawn illustrations that explained how her brain processed numbers differently. She left it on the kitchen table with a sticky note on it saying:

She rushed to her room so she didn't have to watch them read it. Worries danced through her head. What if they thought her story was a waste of time and threw it in the trash? What if they still thought she was just lazy? She started reading to distract herself—finally, in fiction, her mind relaxed.

A little later, her mom called her downstairs. She didn't know what to expect and walked in biting her nails. Her parents sat at the kitchen table, the pages of her story spread open in front of them.

Her mom instructed her to sit opposite her, then said, "Amara, this is very good. You are a talented storyteller."

"Your Mom and I feel we may have been too harsh on you. We don't fully understand, but we are trying," Dad said with a slight smile.

"We are going to do more research so we can understand further." Mom nodded. "You can go on the camping trip, but only if you promise us you will try twice as hard with math from now on," Mom said.

Amara beamed. "Thanks, Mom. I promise."

Although she still struggled with math, Amara discovered new ways to work with numbers, and gradually, she found that she wasn't as scared of them anymore. She knew she would never be a math whiz like the rest of her family, but she was okay with that. All she could do was her best, and that's exactly what she intended to do.

P.S.

For the longest time, I thought struggling with math made me stupid. No matter how hard I tried, the numbers twisted in my head until I felt like a failure. Everyone else seemed to understand algebra and geometry, so why not me? People told me to "listen properly" and "try harder," but that didn't help—I just felt smaller and smaller.

What I finally learned is this: Brains don't all work the same way. Mine mixes up numbers, and that's okay. It doesn't mean I'm lazy or dumb. It just means I need to learn differently. Finding out I have dyscalculia didn't make me weak—it gave me strength, which led to finding answers. And it reminded me that my love for words and stories is a strength, not a flaw.

So if you've ever felt "not enough" because something is harder for you, please know this: You are not broken. You're just you—and that is more than enough.

XOXOX,
Amara

CHAPTER 6

Vera's Family Feud

VERA GRABBED AN APPLE OUT OF the fruit bowl as she started telling her mom all about her day.

"You should have seen me in volleyball practice. I made this one spike so powerful, Leah and Rochelle had to dive out of the way."

Through her words, she heard sniffles across the room. Following the sounds, she noticed her mom sitting at the kitchen table—a cup of black coffee in front of her as she dabbed at her eyes with her shirt sleeve.

"Mom, what's wrong?" Vera asked as she stood in front of the table.

"It's . . . Dad. He's . . . he's gone," Mom cried.

"Gone?" Vera stared at her in confusion. "Gone where?"

"He doesn't live here anymore. No . . . no. Now he lives with . . . *her*." Her mom lifted her cup, but didn't drink from it. Even though a bright pink ceramic flower partly covered her mom's face, Vera noticed teary blobs roll down her cheeks.

That morning, she'd had breakfast with both of her parents and her younger twin brothers, Gus and Dean, as normal. It hadn't even been a full day ago, yet now it felt like an eternity. It turned out, after they left for school, Dad told Mom he was moving in with another woman. Then he packed his bags and left.

Vera checked his office. His files were gone and the desk drawers were empty, but the family photos were still there, snippets of a brighter, happier time.

She felt so confused and didn't understand how her life could change this quickly. At first, she blamed herself. Had she badgered her dad too many times, or had she played her favorite pop album on a constant loop too loudly? Then, she found herself feeling angry. How could he just up and leave them? Her brothers were only seven. They needed their dad around, and they didn't understand why he had left. *She* needed her dad around.

Her mom was either working late to make more money or rushing around to pick the twins up from one of their clubs. So, suddenly, Vera found herself in a vortex of chores, chores, and more chores. She had to do the laundry, clean the kitchen, empty the dishwasher, walk their energetic beagle, Scooter, make the twins' lunches, and also tidy up after them.

There were also multiple occasions when her mom would burst into tears. It happened when they were watching a movie where an animated bunny bought his partner carrots. Then again, when Mom saw a post on social media of Dad on vacation with his new girlfriend.

On these occasions, Vera hugged her mom and then agreed to look after the twins while she had a relaxing bath.

She wanted to help her mom, but it was becoming exhausting. She never seemed to have time for herself anymore, and it was now normal for her to panic-write her homework on the bus.

In geography class, the teacher scowled as he handed her assignment back and muttered, "Vera, this is very disappointing."

She stared at it and gulped. She'd set aside enough time to work on the assignment, but then her arguing brothers had distracted her—there had been a lost toy car emergency.

When her mom returned from overtime, she'd been so exhausted she'd fallen asleep on the couch, so Vera read the twins a bedtime story. By the time she finished it, she was so tired, she ended up falling asleep at her desk and didn't put her work away—a bad idea when Scooter liked to chew anything in sight. She'd had to quickly copy over her already terrible assignment onto a fresh piece of paper.

"You got a D-? Um, Vera, what happened?" her friend Reina asked.

"Nothing." Vera shoved her assignment under her textbook and then forced a smile.

She tried telling herself that it was just some dumb assignment, but then the rest of her grades started slipping too. She just didn't have the time and concentration to study anymore.

Then that weekend, she was supposed to be going to the waterpark with her friends. She'd been excited about it all week, but on Saturday morning, Dad's lawyer emailed Mom about beginning the divorce proceedings, and she was very upset. Vera canceled with her friends so she could be with her mom and also look after her brothers.

On Monday, her friends were annoyed with her for dropping out on them last minute. Worst still, when they finally forgave her, she had to listen to them going on about the different water slides they went on.

Vera couldn't remember the last time she'd felt happy. She definitely couldn't remember the last time her mom had been happy. She worried that now her dad had left, this was her life now. A chaotic, tiring, never-ending misery.

In volleyball practice, she thought about how much she missed her dad, how upset her mom was, how confused her brothers were, and how her best just didn't feel good enough. These thoughts fizzled in her head like a shaken soda can until they all became too much. She missed the serves, her attacks were off-center, and she was so distracted with her thoughts, she didn't see the ball until it whacked her in the face.

After practice, her coach pulled her aside and told her she hadn't been trying hard enough, and warned her that if she didn't start putting in more effort, she could lose her spot on the team. Vera's world seemed to shrink around her. By the time she walked into the locker room, her breathing was frantic and her thoughts had turned gray.

She heard her teammates talking to her, but she couldn't make out their words. They guided her over to a bench and passed her some water.

As she slowly began to calm down and her surroundings unblurred, she overheard her teammate Emilia say, "Talk about being dramatic. She shouldn't be on the team."

Vera grabbed her duffel bag and rushed out of there. She felt like her parents' divorce had made her suck at volleyball—her most favorite thing—and now she'd have to go home and do chores, walk Scooter, console her mom, and look after the twins.

By the time she arrived home, her sadness had transformed into rage.

Then her mom turned to her and *tsk*ed. "Vera, I told you to empty the trash before school. You can't expect me to do everything."

Vera threw her bag on the floor, stomped on it, and screamed, "I don't have volleyball anymore! I don't have

Dad anymore! It's all your fault! I hate you for making him leave!"

Vera saw the hurt look in her mom's eyes. Although she felt bad about it, she found herself kicking her bag across the room and then storming out of the house.

As she walked, it began to rain, weather that matched her mood. Her feet led the way, automatically leading her to Josie's Diner. She slumped into one of the velvet booths and wrapped a strand of her soggy hair around her finger.

She wanted everything to be like it used to be. Her dad always used to bring them to this diner after a volleyball match, or one of the twins' clubs, when they would squish into a booth and order milkshakes. Now the booth felt empty, and Vera felt lonelier than ever. She took her phone out of her pocket and called her dad. He answered on the fifth ring, the sounds of a train station behind him.

"Dad, things are . . . I . . . I miss you," she sobbed.

"Yeah, I miss you and the twins too. I'll see you soon, I promise," he replied in a distracted voice.

"Dad, Mom and I had a fight. Can I come stay—"

"Honey, gotta go. I'll talk to you again soon." He hung up.

As Vera stared at the blank cell phone screen, her heart raced and her vision went fuzzy. She gripped her hands on the edge of the table and let out panicked breaths. She couldn't breathe. She couldn't think. The diner's checkered walls felt like they were closing in on her.

"Vera!" a familiar voice shouted.

She turned around and saw Gus and Dean running over to her. Then, behind them, she saw Mom hurrying over. Her brothers jumped onto the seat next to her.

"Look what Mom got us." Gus waved two toy cars at her.

"They're superfast," Dean said as he whizzed a shiny blue toy car off the table.

The boys laughed, and as the fuzziness started to fade, Vera laughed too.

"Squish in, boys," Mom said, passing Dean his car. "If you play with your cars over there, I'll get you chocolate milkshakes."

Both boys nodded and scooted over so Mom could sit next to Vera. Suddenly, Vera found herself enveloped in a big hug. She smelled her mom's floral perfume and started to feel a little better.

"Sweetie, I'm sorry. It's been tough recently, huh?" Mom said in a quiet voice. "I know I've put too much pressure on you when I shouldn't have. It's a big change for us all, but it will be okay."

"I miss Dad." Vera sniffed, her words muffled in her mom's sweater. "But I miss how things were the most.

I just . . . I can't do it all."

"I know. You're not gonna have to anymore. We're gonna make some changes so it's easier for us all. Boys, you'll help out, won't you?" Mom asked the twins.

They both nodded.

"We're gonna have a chore chart," Gus said.

"If we help out, Mom's gonna buy us all the treats we want," Dean added.

"Not quite." Mom chuckled. "I said we would have a Friday diner treat night, and bowling. Does that sound good?" She smiled at Vera.

Vera smiled back. "Yep. I'm sorry for shouting, Mom. I didn't mean what I said. I just feel so confused, and angry, and sad. I feel like my emotions are trying to suffocate me."

"It's a big change for us all, but we have each other, and that's the most important thing. I promise, it will get easier," Mom said.

After that, they all had milkshakes and sweet treats, and for the first time since Dad left, Vera felt a glimmer of happiness.

Back home, they made a chore chart—that they stuck high on the fridge so Scooter couldn't chew it—and now that they split the house chores, Vera didn't feel so overwhelmed.

She also started practicing yoga with her mom, and

learned some breathing exercises so she could calm herself down when she had panicky moments.

Her grades improved, she always made time for her friends, and also confided in them about how she was feeling—they made a TikTok to cheer her up. She also spoke to her coach, who ended up being extremely understanding of Vera's situation.

Vera still missed having her dad around, and it was hard to adjust to the changes. Despite this, they worked hard to get through their problems as a family. Together, Vera didn't feel so alone. Together, she knew that they could support each other and get through anything.

P.S.

When my dad left, it felt like my whole world cracked. Suddenly, I was juggling chores, looking after my brothers, worrying about my mom, and trying to keep my grades up—all while pretending I was fine. But inside, I wasn't fine at all. I was exhausted, angry, scared, and confused.

Here's what I learned: Families aren't perfect, and sometimes life can throw wild, unexpected, overwhelming curveballs at you. When this happens, leaning on the people who love you makes it easier. When I finally admitted I couldn't do it all, my mom and brothers stepped up. We started sharing the load, and for the first time in a while, I felt lighter.

We still have our ups and downs, but we feel more like a team than ever—including Scooter, who gives the best cuddles and face licks when I'm down.

So if you ever feel crushed by everything on your shoulders, remember: You don't have to handle it by yourself. When times are hard, don't be afraid to ask your friends and family for support. Trust me, they all care about you and want to help.

Lots of love,
Vera

CHAPTER 7

Scarlett Gets a Grip

Scarlett looked in her rose-gold mirror and struck her sassiest pose. Her skin glowed, her hair shone, and her makeup and outfit looked effortlessly perfect. She believed she was a style icon; well, she definitely believed she was the most fashionable girl in school.

She double-checked her reflection in the mirror and grinned proudly. For Scarlett, image was everything. Luckily, her parents both had high-paying jobs, which meant that whatever she wanted, she got. The latest must-have shoes in every color. The in-season purse. The branded lip gloss that influencers were raving about on TikTok.

Scarlett could sense a fashion disaster from a hallway away—it was one of her most cherished skills. Just hearing the *clonk* of cheap shoes, or seeing dirty sneaker trail marks nauseated her. She didn't understand how some people were okay looking a mess.

In the kitchen, she was carefully pouring milk over her

cereal when she noticed her dad was sitting at the table in his pajamas.

Furrowing her eyebrows, she asked, "Um, Dad, why are you dressed like that? Don't you have work?"

There was an awkward silence. It was so uncomfortable that Scarlett—who couldn't stand noisy little kids—longed for her baby brother to start wailing just to fill it.

"Ah, yeah," Dad muttered, staring glumly at his toast. "I . . . I lost my job."

"What!" Scarlett clattered her spoon into her bowl, causing milk to splash over her outfit.

"We were going to talk to you about it later. Your dad will find another job, but until then, we're going to have to make some changes," Mom said.

"What kind of changes?" Scarlett frowned as she dabbed at her shirt with a napkin.

Dad sighed. "I'm sorry, Scarlett, we can't afford to pay your allowance anymore."

"What? No! This is sooo unfair. I didn't do anything. It isn't my fault Dad lost his job, why should I suffer?" She jumped to her feet and threw the napkin onto the table. "How am I supposed to buy clothes and makeup without an allowance?"

"Honey, you have a closet full of outfits to wear," Mom replied.

"You have to be kidding," Scarlett groaned. "I've already worn them. I can't wear them *again*."

"You'll just have to. We need to save our money for bills and food, not clothes and makeup," Dad grunted.

"This is sooo humiliating. I'm Scarlett Valentine. I can't be seen in the same outfit twice!" she screeched at them. "And now, I've gotta change my outfit because you made me spill milk all over it."

Scarlett stormed out of the kitchen and ran up to her bedroom. As she scanned through her overflowing closet for something to wear, she thought about how this was awful . . . terrible . . . catastrophic. Her image was everything. How was she supposed to keep up with all of the latest trends without any money?

Ugh! She was convinced this was the worst day *ever*! She threw on one of her emergency outfits—a ruffled miniskirt and a cute shirt—then she slammed the front door as she left the house.

During study time in the library, Scarlett couldn't stop thinking about her allowance cut. She only had forty dollars left and daydreamed as she tried to work out what she could buy with that. She sighed in frustration. It was useless; the cute pair of jeans she had her eye on was double the cost of that.

"Scarlett, look at Zara's cardigan," Emilia whispered. "Ugh! Looks like she raided her grandma's closet."

"Um . . . oh yeah!" Scarlett muttered, glancing at Zara, but feeling too deflated to respond properly.

Emilia gave her a confused look. "Is something wrong?"

"Yeah, Scarlett, you don't seem yourself," Rochelle said as she peered over her textbook.

"No. I just don't care about Vera's stupid, itchy, smelly old cardigan," she hissed. "And I don't care about depressing poetry either." She threw her books into her backpack, swished her long hair behind her shoulder, and then strutted out of the library.

At lunch, she sat on the bench in the yard and judged the other students' appearances out of ten. Normally, this was one of her favorite things to do, but today, she found herself too preoccupied to care about Amara's ink-stained hands . . . 2/10. Or Nora's food-speckled shirt . . . 1/10.

She folded her arms and mumbled to herself about how unfair her life was. Thanks to her parents, she would probably end up being a walking fashion disaster.

"Hey," Rochelle said as she sat next to her. "You weren't in the cafeteria, so I bought you this." She passed her a sandwich. "It's grilled turkey, no cheese."

"Thanks," she muttered as she took it from her. "But I'm not hungry."

"What's wrong? You've been weird all day."

"My dad lost his job and now I'm freaking out 'cause

my parents aren't gonna give me my allowance anymore. How can I buy the new Dior eyeshadow palette now?" She blew air up at her bangs.

"Oh, that sucks, but you could babysit like I do. That's how I was able to get my new sneakers," Rochelle said as she swirled her foot in the air to emphasize the blue stripe.

Scarlett wrinkled her nose. "Ew! Little kids, no thanks. My brother is bad enough. They're all germ carriers and dirty diapers."

"The kids I look after aren't so bad." She shrugged. "Sometimes I let them stay up late and we watch cartoons and eat popcorn."

Scarlett made an unimpressed face. Stinky kids cuddling up to her with sticky popcorn fingers was a big no!

"Look, you don't have to give them popcorn." Rochelle smiled, knowing her friend all too well. "I could ask around and see if I can get you a job, if you want?"

"I guess, but if one of those brats puts their sticky fingers on my Burberry purse, I'll scream." She tensed up just thinking about it.

"Um, parents don't usually like it when you yell around their kids, so maybe just scream internally."

"Fine. Thanks." She forced a smile.

Later that day, Rochelle messaged Scarlett, telling her she'd found her a babysitting job for that Saturday night.

Scarlett arrived at the house just on time and followed the sound of annoying kids' music into the living room. The boy, Cooper, knelt in front of the coffee table and smashed his toy monster trucks together. While the girl, Alice, stopped making her dolls dance so she could slurp her milkshake.

Everything looked sticky and dirty, and Scarlett tried not to touch any surfaces to save her outfit. The kids' parents were in a hurry to leave, so they quickly told her to help herself to snacks, that bedtime was at eight, and their contact number was on the fridge.

Once the parents left, Scarlett turned the music off and pulled some candy out of her purse. "You can have this if you want."

Cooper grinned and went to grab it, but Scarlett lifted it out of reach. "Nah ah! You only get it if you agree to go to bed and leave me alone."

"But it's only six. Mom said we could stay up till eight," Alice groaned.

"Look! Do you want this candy or not?" She waved it at them.

The kids nodded, so Scarlett found some bowls in the kitchen and split it between them. She shoved the bowls into their hands, shooed them off to bed, then sat on the couch—carefully so she didn't crease her dress—and scrolled through her cell.

About thirty minutes later, she was watching *Project Runway* and remarking to herself on how she could make better outfits, when she heard a sob coming from the doorway. She looked and saw Alice standing there, her face tearstained and her eyes puffy.

"What d'ya want? I don't have any more candy," Scarlett huffed.

"It's not that." Alice sniffed as she shuffled into the room. "You're really pretty and have nice clothes and . . . um . . . the girls at my school are mean about mine."

Scarlett looked at Alice's bunny-face pink pajamas and muttered, "I'm not surprised." As fresh tears rolled down the little girl's face, Scarlett shuddered at how runny-nosed she was. "Ugh! Enough already. If I agree to help you, will you stop blubbering?"

The girl wiped her nose on her sleeve and then nodded. Scarlett handed her a tissue and then got to work. Looking through Alice's closet, she saw a lot of pastel dresses and plain sweaters. Okay, so her clothes were on the bland side, but they weren't totally awful or anything.

"So what mean stuff do the girls say?" Scarlett asked as she pulled out a lilac dress and laid it on the bed.

"My clothes are babyish and boring." Her bottom lip trembled as she spoke.

"Hey, no more tears." Scarlett waved a finger at her. "Besides, we can totally sparkle up this dress, but keep it easy to wash so your mom doesn't freak out."

Scarlett took her fabric glue and fabric scraps out of her purse—she always carried them around with her in case of a fashion emergency. Then, she also looked in Alice's arts and crafts box and found sequins and miniature bows.

Using the scrunchie around her wrist, she tied her hair up—a must-do when she was in design mode—and then got to work gluing a glittery ribbon trim to the dress. She didn't stop there, and also jazzed up some bland T-shirts and boring sweaters.

With the hall as her runway, Alice showed off her new outfits while Scarlett clapped and said, "Woohoo, you go, girl!"

Alice's sad face transformed into a smile, and she ran over to Scarlett and wrapped her arms around her. Scarlett stood rigid. She wasn't used to anyone hugging her, let alone a sticky-fingered little kid. Despite this, she found herself smiling too. She'd had fun helping Alice, and she felt good seeing how happy she was.

"Okay, enough. Keep your snotty fingers away from me."

Alice stuck her hands out as she continued to hug her.

When Alice went to bed, Scarlett went downstairs and started sketching. On seeing how these hurtful comments affected Alice, she reflected on some of the mean comments she had made to other people.

The reason she loved fashion so much was because it allowed for creative freedom and interpretation. Being unkind about the way people chose to dress wasn't the kind of fashion designer she wanted to be.

This gave her an amazing idea, so she started sketching T-shirt designs to suit different personalities. She continued babysitting so she could fund her idea and turn her designs into actual T-shirts, which she started selling online. This was a great way to begin her fashion designer career and also make some extra money.

She made her parents T-shirts—her way of apologizing—and also gave free ones to some of the girls she'd been mean to at school. One with a cute ink squiggle design for Amara, and a dark one with a colorful swirl trim for Nora—great for disguising food stains.

Scarlett still had her opinions about the way other people dressed, but she wasn't so quick to say mean things about them anymore. Instead, she kept her opinions to herself and only said something when it was a compliment that she actually meant.

P.S.

I used to think fashion was about one thing: looking perfect. The right shoes, the right bag, the right lip gloss. And if someone didn't measure up? I'd roll my eyes or say something snarky. I thought that my mood could be determined by how cute I looked. It was only when I had to work to be able to buy what I wanted that I realized something important: Style isn't about perfection, it's about expression. Clothes tell our stories, and no one's story deserves to be mocked.

When I helped a little girl who felt "boring" in her outfits, I saw how powerful kindness (and a little creativity) could be. Fashion shouldn't tear people down —it should lift them up. Now, I design pieces that celebrate personality instead of criticizing it.

So here's my advice: Wear what makes you feel amazing, not what someone else says you should. And if you do comment on someone's style, make it kind and real. If we all wore the same outfits, it would be totally boring! Be you and never let anyone dull your spark.

C-ya,
Scarlett

CHAPTER 8

Reina's Game Over!

Reina's one true love in life was video games. She adored them all—adventure, cozy, competitive, puzzle, strategy. She would play any game at least once.

Her love of gaming began at four years old when she was visiting family in Japan. She didn't speak Japanese, and her cousin barely spoke any English, but they found a way of communicating through a Nintendo game where they raised miniature fluffy monsters.

Now at fifteen, gaming was everything. Gaming-related posters covered her bedroom walls and gaming stickers covered her stationery and school books.

Reina's mom was fine with her gaming—provided she kept her grades high. This had all been okay until recently, when a brand-new world-play game called War Quest came out. When she first started playing it, her parents had been arguing all the time, her brother had moved out, and she had been arguing with her friends.

Even though life calmed down, she found herself thinking about this game all the time. In class, she daydreamed about what clothes she should dress her character in, which items she should buy, and which missions she should complete next.

Gaming and just thinking about gaming made her feel like she could take on the world. She turned down hanging out with Amara at the mall and canceled going to the diner with Vera. All so she could rush home from school and play War Quest.

Time seemed to race by when she cast magic spells and roamed enchanted lands. She told herself she'd play for *ten more minutes*, but then ten minutes became another, then another. Suddenly, it was the early hours of the morning, and she hadn't done her schoolwork.

The next day, she panic-wrote her homework during recess. Even though she knew she could have gotten a much higher grade if she'd tried harder, all she could think about was going home and playing War Quest.

The problem was that, due to her slipping grades, her homeroom teacher called her mom to tell her. Reina arrived home to find tape all over her computer and the power cord removed.

"You have to do your schoolwork. Improve your grades and you can have your cord back," her mom said.

"This isn't fair!" Reina groaned, stomping her feet. "You know how important gaming is to me. Besides, I need my computer for doing homework."

"You have your phone if you need the internet, and there's the school library. You need to focus on your schoolwork first and gaming second," Dad insisted.

She rolled her eyes. "Reina, stop with the attitude and just focus on your studies." Mom glowered.

She waited until they left her room and then pulled a spare cord out from the box under her bed. Her parents knew nothing about gaming at all, so she thought it was so easy to continue playing games without their knowledge. She did feel a little bit bad that she was disobeying them, but she also felt they were being unfair in expecting her not to game. Gaming was everything to her; she couldn't just go cold turkey on it.

That night, she tiptoed over to her computer, removed the tape, plugged in the spare cord, muted the sound, and then stayed up most of the night gaming. When she found her eyes shutting or herself yawning, she ate candy to give her a sugar burst. She also bought some energy drinks and drank them to stay awake.

The next morning, she made sure she removed the cord, replaced the tape, and hid all evidence of her unhealthy snacking.

At school, she handed in her homework late, was moody

with her friends, and found it impossible to concentrate. She almost blew up the science lab by adding the wrong substance into her beaker, earning her a week's worth of detentions. Then, when Vera was trying to talk to her about something important, Reina zoned out—Vera thought she was purposely being rude, and they argued.

Even though she felt sad, all she could think about was logging into the game. Playing War Quest would make her forget about her problems. It would make everything seem better.

The next day at school, she failed her history test. She shoved the paper into her locker, sat by herself at lunch, and daydreamed about her game.

She stayed up all night, ate five candy bars, and drank three energy drinks. The next day, she was so tired she could barely keep her eyes open. On the walk to school, she bashed into a tree and ended up with a huge bruise on her forehead.

This only made her mood worse. She was mumbling to herself as she tried to find a textbook in her backpack when Amara came over to her.

"Oh wow, that's a shiner. What happened?" She pointed at Reina's forehead.

"Stop making fun of me. It's not like you're perfect. At least *I* know how to find the lowest common denominator correctly!" she snapped.

"I'm . . . I'm not . . ." Amara stammered and then turned to walk off.

Reina knew her friend had dyscalculia and struggled with numbers, so this was a mean thing to say. Even though she felt bad about it, she was too tired to figure out how to make it right. Instead, she focused on War Quest and what quests she would go on later. As she thought about this, the world seemed very real to her. She was seeing the game world through her character and could touch the long blades of grass and see a small, fluffy monster rolling in it. She stared at it, confused. It was one of the monsters from the game she played with her cousin as a kid.

"Huh! You're not from this game," she remarked.

She heard laughter around her and jerked forward—she wasn't in War Quest anymore. She was at her desk, her arms half dangling off, and her class notes stuck to her face.

The laughter seemed to whirl around her and she wanted to melt away from the shame. She had never fallen asleep in class before, and it was something she definitely didn't want to do again.

Her teacher made her stay behind, told her how disappointed he was in her, and gave her detention.

Although this annoyed Reina, she convinced herself it was okay, as it could have been worse. Then she walked out of class and saw everyone staring at their cell phones, laughing, then pointing at her.

"I'd check your phone if I were you." Emilia grinned as she walked past.

Reina's heart thudded as she reached into the front of her backpack and pulled out her cell. Someone had secretly filmed her asleep in class and sent it to the entire school! She watched on in embarrassment as she saw herself snore, sleep talk, almost tumble off her desk, then wake up with the paper stuck to her face.

Vera came over and asked if she was okay, but Reina ignored her and rushed to the bathroom. She was too tired to deal with her friends, or teasing, or anything else. She stayed silent for the rest of the day and did the best she could to remain awake in class.

Back home, she went right to bed and fell asleep. Then the next morning, when she woke up, her head felt clearer. She took her spare power cord downstairs and handed it to her mom.

As her mom started to speak, Reina blurted out, "I lied. I've been gaming all along, and I can't do it anymore. I'm tired, moody, my skin is covered in pimples, I was mean to my friends, I failed my test, and I'm all over the internet looking like a loser!"

She thought her mom would get mad, but to her surprise, she walked over to Reina and hugged her.

They talked about video games and how playing them in moderation was fine, but how letting them take over and rule your life wasn't. Together, her mom helped her make fruit smoothies and healthy oatmeal cookies. She stopped the candy and energy drinks, drank more water, and started going for walks and exercising to clear her mind.

It was hard sometimes, especially at night when her computer seemed to call to her. She ended up placing a blanket over it, and eventually, she managed to stop thinking about War Quest and fall asleep.

She focused on her studies and getting her grades up. Bought her friends cupcakes as an apology and told them she wouldn't be such a mean idiot again. Joined the chess team so she could game without getting screen blur—it turned out she was great at it. And prioritized reality over fantasy worlds.

By having a break from gaming, she found herself embracing how amazing reality could be. She went on mini quests with her friends through the woods and collected acorns and odd-shaped leaves, and found that being in nature could be far more fun than being in a digital one.

When she walked into her room, saw the tape removed from her computer, and the power cord returned, she smiled to herself, but she also felt a little nervous. She missed gaming, but worried she would become addicted again.

She completed her chores, finished her homework, messaged her friends, and then allocated herself an hour of game time. As she sat at her computer, she saw a sticky note on her keyboard that she'd missed before:

> Remember that
> gaming is fun,
> but reality
> is better.

She smiled to herself, recognizing her mom's writing and knowing she was right. Taking a deep breath, Reina set a timer on her cell phone for an hour, switched on her computer, and felt a buzz of excitement as she watched the game load.

She chewed on an oatmeal cookie and then started to game. As she saw it, life was kinda like one big game. Taking care of herself helped her level up and led her to get the most enjoyment out of her day.

P.S.

I love video games. They're exciting, magical, and sometimes even feel more real than reality. But here's the thing: I let gaming take over my life. I stayed up too late, snapped at my friends, failed tests, and basically turned into a tired, grumpy game villain. Worst of all, I forgot that life outside the screen mattered too.

What I learned is this: Gaming can be awesome, but balance is everything. An hour of playing is fun; ten hours straight just makes you miserable. Quests in games are cool, but quests in real life—like laughing with friends, exploring a cool new place, or even just eating cookies with your mom—are even better.

So keep gaming if you love it. Just don't forget the real world is waiting for you. That's where the best memories are made.

Peace out,
Reina

CHAPTER 9

Zara's Crush Rush

Zara straightened her daisy-patterned headband and blushed as she looked at Zac. She had been friends with him since kindergarten and, for as long as she could remember, she'd had a crush on him.

The problem was that it was becoming harder to keep her feelings a secret. She wasn't sure when her inability to act normally around Zac started exactly. It had been a series of little things that all added up: turning bright red when he invited her on a group trip to the movies; getting word vomit when she tried to ask him to pass the mayo; making awkward faces when he asked her for the time.

Although Zac seemed oblivious to this, Nora, Leah, and Florence noticed.

At school, when Zara tripped over her own feet because she was so busy looking over at Zac, Nora said, "Plllleassse, will you just tell him how you feel already."

Zara shook her head. *Nope! No way!* The thought of

being rejected was scarier than the last horror movie she'd watched to impress Zac—resulting in her sleeping with the lights on for a whole week. Unlike Nora, who'd just started dating Elijah, Zara had never had a boyfriend before. She had no idea how she was supposed to act around Zac, but most of all, she was afraid of blurting out her feelings just for him to laugh in her face.

"Don't be silly. Besides, he doesn't like me like that." Zara shrugged, trying to downplay her feelings.

"You don't know that," Nora replied. "Actually, I think you would make a cute couple."

Zara couldn't hide her smile. She thought that they'd make a cute couple too.

Nora grinned. "Your couple name could be Zaca. It's a Z-name match in heaven."

Although Zara play-hit her friend's arm, the more she thought about it, the more she dared to imagine that Zac might like her too. She decided that maybe, just maybe, she should open up and tell him how she really felt.

As she walked home with her friends, she found herself blurting out, "I like Zac, but I don't know how to tell him."

"I knew it." Leah grinned.

"Ooh, I know. Tell him at the funfair," Florence suggested.

"Funfair? Oh, you mean the state fair." Nora having to

decipher Florence's British words and phrases was something she was used to.

"Yeah, you said there's a fair there, right? So it's a funfair," Florence confirmed. "You could confess your feelings, and he could win you a teddy on the hook-a-duck. It sounds sooo romantic."

"Ew, cringe fest." Leah scrunched up her face.

"I agree with Flo. It sounds romantic. Are you going to do it, Zara?" Nora looked at her.

To Zara's surprise, she found herself nodding. As her friends squealed and grabbed her arms, her thoughts were spinning. She had been friends with Zac for forever, but this was the first time she dared to believe that maybe they could be something more.

All week, Zara planned her outfit, makeup, and practiced her confession speech to Oscar, her giant stuffed bear—a silent but squishy stand-in for Zac.

She arrived at the fair in a hot pink skirt that matched her hair ties, and went on a couple of rides with her friends to calm her nerves—bad idea! The Tilt-A-Whirl made her stomach lurch.

She was trying her best not to throw up when she heard a, "BOO!" as hands gripped her shoulders. Spinning around, she saw Zac grinning at her, pink cotton candy stuck to the corner of his mouth.

"Jerk." Leah glared at him. "You shouldn't scare someone who's been on a ride. You could get barfed on."

He shrugged. "I'll take my chances."

Leah winked at Zara before she grabbed Nora's and Florence's hands and led them off to get corn dogs. Alone with Zac, Zara felt herself blushing, and when she tried to talk, strange sounds came out instead of words.

"Hey, Zara, are you okay?" he asked.

"Y-yeah." She squeaked and coughed to clear her voice. "Yes. Good, all good. You?"

"Yeah, I'm great. Um, I have something to tell you, actually." He scratched his head.

Zara's heart fluttered. He was looking at her with such intensity, and she was sure she felt a spark between them. She knew it was now or never. She took a deep breath, tightened one of her hair ties, and started telling him how she felt.

She'd just opened her mouth when she saw a sparkle in Zac's blue eyes. Only, he wasn't looking at her. He was looking behind her. She turned around to see what he was looking at and stopped dead. Walking toward her with a giant stuffed tiger in her arms was Scarlett.

She told herself there must have been some mistake, but to her horror, Scarlett walked over to Zac, used a glittery pink fingernail to scrape the cotton candy off the corner of his mouth, and then kissed him on the lips.

Zara stared open-mouthed at them. Her heart sank and her skin itched. She felt like she was back on the Tilt-A-Whirl, only this time she was whizzing at superspeed.

"Y-you two are a-a . . . oh!" she stammered.

"Yep, we've been dating for a few weeks, but this is our first public appearance," Scarlett said as she clung to Zac's arm. As she tried her best to process this nightmare scenario, Zara's gaze stopped on the giant tiger. "Cute, isn't it? Although it does smell kinda funky." Scarlett shook it so its tail flopped. "Zac won it for me on the ring toss. Turns out he has a mean throw."

"Yes. Cute," Zara somehow managed to say, even though inside, her heart felt like it was cracking. "I have to go."

She pointed at nothing in particular, forced back tears, then rushed off. Her friends saw her leave and shouted after her, but she didn't stop. She worried that if she did, her heartache would freeze her to the spot, and that with it, she'd never unfreeze again.

Once home, she smelled her mom's fresh-baked sour cherry cake—a taste of their Persian heritage, and Zara's absolute favorite food—but she was so upset, she rushed upstairs and into her bedroom.

She wrapped her arms around Oscar and cried into his fur. Her heart ached so badly, and she couldn't stop picturing Scarlett and Zac kissing and holding hands.

"Of course he wouldn't like you like that. You're a stupid loser," she taunted herself. This caused her to sob more and turn Oscar's fur damp and sticky.

Her friends tried messaging her to ask if she was okay, but she ignored them. She wasn't ready to talk about it; it hurt far too much.

She couldn't help but look through group pictures of her and Zac. One of him with that big stupid grin of his that she secretly adored. One of him with his arm around her. One of them both making dumb faces.

There was a knock at the door, and thinking it was her mom, she said, "I don't want cake. I just wanna be left alone."

There was another knock, then the door creaked open, and Nora peeked in.

"How about cake with ice cream?" She opened the door farther, and Leah and Florence walked in holding a bowl of sour cherry cake and a tub of chocolate brownie ice cream.

Zara managed a smile and beckoned them over. They all sat on her bed and ate the cake and ice cream. Knowing her friends had left the fair early to check on her made Zara feel a little better—even though her heart still pined for Zac.

"We didn't know he was with Scarlett," Nora said.

"Yeah, I didn't see that one coming," Leah added.

"It makes sense. She's pretty and popular, and it's fine. He can date who he wants." Zara sighed.

"She did ask if you were okay. Zac did too," Florence said.

On the mention of his name, Zara's heart flipped. She fell silent as she looked at her cell and saw the worried message from him:

Zara, are u OK? Did something happen? Pls let me know ur safe.

A line of worried face emojis followed. Zara looked at them and exhaled. She knew he cared about her as a friend, but right now it felt too raw to think about friendship. She put her cell phone down and leaned her head on Leah's shoulder.

She sighed. "I feel like my heart will never heal."

"It will." Leah pressed her hand to Zara's. "In the meantime, we can totally ignore Zac if you want."

Nora gave a horrified look and fiddled with her glasses and Florence looked down at her bracelet, but neither said anything.

"No. He hasn't done anything wrong. I want you to stay friends with him." Zara nodded. "I want to be his friend too. I just need time."

The next few weeks were hard for Zara. Every time she saw Zac with Scarlett, she felt sick and quickly ran off the other way. Whenever he tried talking to her alone, she pretended she hadn't heard him or quickly made an excuse to leave. She never replied to any of his messages, and when he joined them for lunch, she avoided eye contact with him and then scuttled off when the conversation turned away from her.

She felt bad, as she knew he hadn't actually done anything wrong. He liked Scarlett in that way, not her, and as much as this hurt, it's just how it was. She knew her actions were making it hard for her other friends to hang around with Zac. They told her how he kept asking them what was wrong with her and if he had upset her in some way.

On one occasion, she was sorting out her locker when she heard her name being called behind her. Her heart fell; she recognized that voice. She turned to see Zac standing there, a concerned look on his face.

"Hey, Zara, did I do something? You've been weird since the fair, and I don't get why."

"No." She hugged her textbook. "I . . . I have class."

"Yeah. Right. Okay." He stared down at his sneakers.

Zara felt bad for how distant and standoffish she'd been around him. She also really missed having him as a friend. She decided that if she couldn't have him as her boyfriend, then she at least wanted him as her friend.

That evening, she helped her mom make a sour cherry cake, then she took a tub of it into school the next day. As the lunch bell rang, she looked at her friends for support before she checked her glittery headband was straight, then walked over to Zac and Scarlett in the hall—she was making him hold her backpack while she applied lip gloss in the mirror on the inside of her locker door.

"Hi. Um, I was wondering if you'd like to join us for lunch. I have cake." She smiled as she waved the tub at them.

Scarlett puckered her lips then said, "Sure. It's not covered in frosting, is it?"

"Great. And nope, no frosting," Zara replied.

"It's sour cherry cake, isn't it?" Zac grinned as he looked at the tub. "Awesome. This cake is dope."

Scarlett and Zac held hands as Zara walked alongside them. Her friends smiled over at her and then joined them. Together, they all walked to the cafeteria.

Although Zara's heart wasn't fully healed, it also didn't ache as much anymore. She was happy that she had some amazing friends in her life and that Zac was still one of them. She was also proud of herself in the end for managing to handle her heartbreak in a grown-up way.

P.S.

I thought telling Zac how I felt would be the scariest thing ever—but it turned out, watching him kiss someone else was way worse. My heart ached so much I thought it would never heal. For weeks, I avoided him and told myself I'd lost not just a crush, but a friend too.

What I finally realized is this: Heartbreak really hurts. It's far worse than stepping on a wasp or accidentally deleting the assignment you spent a month working on. But this feeling doesn't last forever. You can miss someone, even want more than friendship, and still choose to value the bond you already share. I couldn't make Zac like me back in that way, but I could choose to keep him in my life.

So if you ever find yourself crushed by rejection, please know—it doesn't mean you're unworthy. It just means your story isn't with that person. Lean on your friends, give yourself time, and when you're ready, let your heart heal.

Take care,
Zara

CHAPTER 10

Emilia's Failing Feeling

EMILIA DANCED AROUND HER BEDROOM and sang into her hairbrush. Her sister, Mónica, banged on the wall that separated their bedrooms—her way of telling Emilia to shut up.

In typical Emilia fashion, this only made her crank up her volume and she jumped across her room. Another *thud* sounded through the wall, and Emilia ignored it and smirked at her phone—she was recording this for a TikTok.

Ever since Emilia had been six and watched *The Lion King* on Broadway, she had dreamed of being a performer. The stage was where she came alive, and she was convinced she was destined to be a famous actress.

The locked door handle rattled, followed by more enraged knocks.

"Some of us have finals to study for!" Mónica screeched. "If you keep on being this annoying, I'll put glue on your straighteners."

Emilia rolled her eyes and watched her video back. Her sister's threats didn't bother her as she knew her mom would ground her for a year if she carried them out.

She had her own TikTok channel: *EmiliaStarDaze,* in which she reenacted famous TV show and movie scenes. Wednesday had been her last one, and with over two hundred thousand views, it'd proven popular.

At school, she was thinking about what video she should film next when she spotted a group of students standing around the bulletin board. She barged past them to see what they were so fascinated by, and her eyes lit up.

The school was putting on a production of *Grease*, and auditions were tomorrow. She snatched a pen off the girl beside her so she could sign up to try out for the lead role.

Emilia was so certain she would get the part of Sandy, she spent all of lunch quoting her lines. That afternoon when she got home, she pinned back her hair, donned a pink jacket, and recorded a *Grease* medley for her channel—resulting in more wall thuds from Mónica.

During dinner, as Mónica gave her evil looks across the kitchen, their mom noticed and said, "Girls, what's happened now?"

"Ask her. I'm trying to study, and her shrieking is making my eyes bleed," Mónica snarled.

"It's not shrieking. Besides, I need to practice for the school play."

"Oh, do you have a part?" Mom asked.

Emilia was about to explain that auditions were tomorrow, but as she saw it, why bother? It was obvious the lead role was going to be hers.

"Yep, I'm Sandy in *Grease*. It's next month, you should come. I suppose you can come too, Mónica." She smirked at her sister.

She knew what she was saying was risky, but it wasn't a lie if it was a sure thing, right?

Mom clapped. "That's wonderful, isn't it, Mónica?"

"I guess so." Mónica sighed. "Just please keep the noise to a minimum."

"I can't wait to invite all of the family, the neighbors, oh, and Heather and Bob will want to come too." Her mom beamed with pride.

"Yeah. Great," Emilia muttered as she ate a forkful of her enchilada.

It was okay. She was going to get the part anyway, so why wait to tell everyone? Still, she couldn't quite shake an uneasy feeling from her gut.

The auditions went amazingly, and everyone else agreed—students she didn't even know tapped her on the shoulder, gave her a thumbs-up, and told her that she'd smashed the audition.

Emilia couldn't wait to dazzle on stage in front of the

whole school. She thought about her choreography and how she could put her own stamp on it.

On hearing a student mention that the roles were posted, Emilia grabbed Scarlett's arm and dragged her over to the bulletin board. On seeing her, there was a deathly silence around the board, and everyone stared at her.

"What're you looking at?" she groaned at some girl whose name she didn't know.

Through the gathering of students, she saw exactly why they were reacting this way. Next to the role of Sandy wasn't her name. Instead, written there was the name Florence Kennedy.

"WHAT!" Emilia tore the paper off the board and stared at it. "This has to be a joke. I've had sports socks in my backpack longer than *she's* been at this school. Not that I don't wash them or anything. She doesn't even speak properly. She has that stupid accent."

The rage continued, and Scarlett had to pull her friend into an empty classroom before she got into trouble.

"This is sooo unfair. No one understands what Florence is saying, and she sings like a croaky frog, but hey, at least you get to be understudy," Scarlett tried reassuring her.

"I got *what*?!" Emilia's mouth dropped. She'd been so upset about not getting the part, she hadn't even noticed that. "I'm *no one's* backup. This is a complete joke!"

Scarlett gritted her teeth as she tried and failed to calm Emilia down. She swung her arms in the air and ranted about how Florence's parents must have bribed the teacher. She just couldn't accept that anyone else, especially Florence, deserved the lead role over her.

Emilia tried to forget about it. She refused to show up for rehearsals—no way was she watching Florence prance around performing a part she was born to play. At home, she didn't mention it to her mom and sister and hoped they would have forgotten about it. Yeah, right! It was the first thing her mom mentioned when she arrived home from work.

Emilia thought about telling her the truth, but as she tried to, she saw her mom's delighted face and just couldn't get the words out. Worst of all, her mom hadn't been kidding about inviting *everyone* to the show. She'd even invited the annoying neighbors two doors down.

If she ignored the problem, it would go away, right? Her mom probably wouldn't be able to get tickets for that many people anyway. Or they probably only said they were coming to be polite, and wouldn't actually show up.

The problem was that posters and advertisements were everywhere. She couldn't turn a corner at school or flick through her social media pages without seeing something about it. There'd even been a flyer sent in her mailbox about it—to her dismay, her mom had used magnets to stick it to the fridge.

She didn't feel much like singing or dancing, and tried distracting herself with trigonometry, which she hated.

She was looking at her math textbook and thinking how much this sucked when she heard a *thud* on the other side of her bedroom wall.

Rolling her eyes, she shouted, "What! I'm not making any noise."

Footsteps followed, and then Mónica barged into her room—blast! She'd forgotten to lock the door.

"Ugh! Get out," Emilia grunted.

"Why aren't you screeching like a coyote?" Mónica looked from her sister to her math homework. "I thought you'd be practicing before your big performance, not studying trig."

"I need to rest my voice. Now get out of my room!" She threw a pen at her sister—it missed.

Mónica looked unconvinced, but Emilia showed her out, twisting the lock on the doorknob.

She didn't know what to do. Tomorrow, the school hall would be full of people who expected to see her in the lead role. What were they going to think when Florence appeared instead, and she didn't have a role at all? Not even one single word.

Emilia hoped that tomorrow would never arrive, but of course, this didn't happen, and she woke up knowing she was in one big mess. She felt so nervous all day, she barely said a word—which was very out of character for her. She stayed late at school to help set up the hall, then, as soon as the audience started showing up, she scuttled into the dressing room to avoid seeing her mom, family, and neighbors.

She sat on a pile of old curtains and thought about how disappointed her mom would be that she lied. Suddenly, she heard muffled sounds coming from somewhere. She traced the sounds to the store cupboard and opened the door to find Florence curled up there, sobbing into her blonde wig.

"Uh, why are you hiding here?" Emilia asked.

"I can't do it. I'm too scared. What if everyone laughs at my accent, or throws stuff at me?" She sobbed some more. "I'm just not good enough."

Emilia stepped over a mannequin and some stinky old costumes so she could sit next to Florence. "I don't wanna sound mean or anything, but I don't think you're right for this role. You don't wanna embarrass yourself out there in front of all of those people, do you?" Florence shook her head and shuddered. "It's okay, I know how to fix this." She gave a sly smile. "I can perform instead. I know all of the lines anyway."

Florence was feeling so nervous that she agreed to this, and she reluctantly handed Emilia her pink jacket. She held the wig out to her as well, but Emilia wrinkled her nose at this and said it was about time Sandy had dark hair instead.

On hearing panicked shouts that it was five minutes until curtain call, she closed the door on Florence and rushed to the stage. Only, the closer she got to it, the guiltier she felt. She wanted to be the lead role, but not like this.

As the boy playing Danny asked her why she was holding Florence's jacket, she mumbled how she needed to give it to her, then hurried off.

Florence was still hiding in the store cupboard, but she had stopped crying. Emilia grabbed her arm, and pulling her to her feet, said, "Florence, you need to go on stage, *now*!"

"B-b-but, I'm too nerv—"

"You can do it. You *will* do it. And you will be amazing. Now get your butt out there and sing your English heart out."

She led Florence toward the stage, tucked her red hair into the wig, then gave her a gentle push out for everyone to see. Emilia watched from the side, smiling as Florence nailed her performance.

Then she looked at the audience and saw her mom's and sister's confused faces in the front row. She knew she'd have to explain what'd happened eventually, but she was dreading doing it.

After the show, Florence came over to her and said, "Thank you for before. I couldn't have done it without you."

Emilia mumbled, "Yeah, no problem."

Her eyes scanned past Florence and to her mom, who looked like she was trying to explain Emilia's no-show in the play to their relatives and neighbors.

"Every actress has their challenges," Emilia told herself as she walked over to them.

Although it was hard, she told the truth about the show and how she'd never been given the lead role. Her mom was disappointed in her, and the embarrassment soared through her body, but she also felt relief that she didn't have to lie anymore.

That night, as she lay in bed and scrolled through TikTok, she heard a *thud* coming from the other side of the bedroom wall. Shortly afterward, her door creaked open and Mónica appeared, leaning in the doorway.

"Lying isn't cool, you know. You upset Mom." She frowned.

"I know," Emilia muttered, not looking away from her cell phone screen.

"Your friends told me you didn't try out for another

role. That was dumb, you would have made a pretty good Rizzo," she said.

"Only pretty good?" Emilia pouted playfully.

Mónica laughed as she gave a half wave and then left the room. As Emilia watched the door close, she knew that her sister was right. She'd been so set on the main role that she'd missed out on the opportunity to try out for one of the other parts.

She never assumed anything was hers again before she had truly earned it. She also refused to limit herself like that again, and she made a promise with herself that from now on, however disappointed she was, she would always smile, stay strong, be graceful in defeat, and keep on trying.

P.S.

I used to believe I was destined to be the star of every stage. I thought I was the best and that was it, which is exactly why I told people I'd landed a lead role before auditions even happened. Hey, I was so sure it would be mine. But when it wasn't, I lied, sulked, and almost ruined everything.

Here's what I learned: Talent matters, yes—but so does honesty, humility, and resilience. You can't assume the spotlight will always shine on you, and you definitely can't force it. What you can do is keep showing up, giving your best, and cheering others on—even when it stings.

Sometimes you'll win the lead and sometimes you won't. Both moments shape you. Losing doesn't mean you've failed—it means you've got another chance to grow, to try again, and to shine brighter next time.

So keep dreaming big—but remember, every amazing actress has experienced rejection. Being graceful in defeat is just as powerful as victory.

Adios for now,
Emilia

PPS.

Through Nora, Florence, Rochelle, Leah, Amara, Vera, Scarlett, Reina, Zara, and Emilia, you've seen how tough growing up can feel. Fear, loneliness, heartbreak, and pressure can be heavy—but you don't have to carry it alone. Asking for help is brave.

If you're struggling, please reach out to someone you trust —family, a teacher, a counselor, or a close friend. And know that confidential, professional support is always there for you:

- US: 988 Suicide & Crisis Lifeline – www.988lifeline.org – call or text 988
- UK: Childline – www.childline.org.uk – call 0800 1111
- Canada: Kids Help Phone – www.kidshelpphone.ca – call or text 988
- Australia: Kids Helpline – www.kidshelpline.com.au – call 1800 55 1800

You are worthy of love, care, and brighter days ahead. Please take the first step and reach out—you are never truly alone.

With love,
The Girls & the Author

Each book that we have published has **a free audio version available.** To download the audiobook for *P.S. You Are Amazing*, **all you have to do is scan the QR code** or visit: www.littlebigpage.com/psamazing

If you have any problems or questions, feel free to contact us at help@littlebigpage.com

Made in United States
North Haven, CT
23 November 2025

82858611R00067